A Sweetheart for Valentine

Lorna Balian

Abingdon Press   Nashville

The small village of St. Valentine woke up most mornings

Library of Congress Cataloging in Publication Data

BALIAN, LORNA
    A sweetheart for Valentine.
    SUMMARY: When a large baby in a large basket is left on the
    steps of the St. Valentine village hall, the villagers decide that
    she will belong to all of them and they name her Valentine.
    [1. St. Valentine's Day—Fiction] I. Title.
    PZ7.B1978Sx   [E]   79-9924

ISBN 0-687-37109-0

Previously published under ISBN 0–687-40771-0 and
ISBN 0-687-40772-9

MANUFACTURED BY THE PARTHENON PRESS AT
NASHVILLE, TENNESSEE, UNITED STATES OF AMERICA

to the crowing of roosters and the gentle lowing of cows anxious to be milked.

For Myrtle — one of my mothers — with love

But one morning a loud howling noise roused all the villagers from their cozy beds.

They came scurrying from all directions to find out what was causing the disturbance.

It was hardly to be believed!
There—on the steps of the village hall—
was a large basket.
And in the basket was a blanket.
And wrapped in the blanket
was a red-faced, bawling baby girl!

She belonged to no one, the poor dear,
so it was decided she would belong to everyone.
Because the whole village of St. Valentine adopted her,
she was named Valentine.

Valentine—right then and there—
had one great-grandfather,
three great-grandmothers,
six grandfathers,
seven grandmothers,
eleven fathers,
eleven mothers,
and more brothers and sisters
than anyone had ever bothered to count.

And it was a good thing too—
Valentine needed a lot of attention.
She ate more than anyone in the village!

The more she ate, the bigger she grew,
and the larger she became, the more she ate,
until she was eating more than everyone in the village.

Great-grandfather called a special meeting.
"Valentine is getting much too big.
We're feeding her too much!" he said.
"She's just a growing child," said her mothers.
"She certainly is!" said her fathers.
"She bawls so loud when she's hungry
that it hurts our ears," said her brothers and sisters.
"We'll have to plant bigger gardens," said her grandparents.
So they did.

Valentine outgrew all the clothes in the village.

Great-grandfather called a special meeting.
"Valentine can't traipse around in her birthday suit!
She'll catch cold," he said.
"We'll try to sew her a dress that's large enough,"
said her mothers.
"Where will we get that much fabric?" asked her fathers.
"We'll use all the scraps in the village,"
said her grandmothers.
"Patchwork might be pretty," said her grandfathers.
"If she doesn't have to wear underwear,
we don't either!" said her brothers and sisters.
"Forget the underwear," said her grandmothers.
So they did.

Valentine got stuck
half in and half out
of the doorway in the village hall.

Great-grandfather called a special meeting.
"Valentine needs a house of her own.
What can we build it with?" he asked.
"She needs a house that will grow as she grows,"
said her mothers.
"That's impossible!" said her fathers,
"There is no way to build a growing house!"
"With vines," said her grandmothers.
"And sunflowers," said her grandfathers.
"We'll plant it," said her brothers and sisters.
So they did.

Valentine grew along with her house.

She became a lovely young lady

with a sweet disposition.

Her brothers and sisters grew too.

They found sweethearts,

got married,

and had babies.

Valentine became lonely.

She longed for someone of her own.

Great-grandfather called a special meeting.

"Valentine needs a sweetheart," he said.

"With her great beauty, that shouldn't be a problem,"

said her mothers, "but it is."

"Many young men love Valentine,

but not one is big enough to carry her off," said her fathers.

"She may never marry," said her grandmothers.

"Probably not," said her grandfathers.

"Too bad," said her brothers and sisters.

Valentine wept.
The village was flooded with tears.

Early one morning a loud crash and a howling noise
roused all the villagers from their cozy beds.
They came scurrying from all directions
to find out what was causing the disturbance.

It was hardly to be believed!
There, stuck in the mud
in the middle of the village,
was a very large, yowling young man!

"I think you have broken your toe, young man,"
said Great-grandfather.
"Why are you wandering around in the dark?"

"I've been walking night and day,
uphill and downhill,
looking for a wife," said the young man.

"Well, well! This is your lucky day!
Our Valentine would be just the girl for you,"
beamed Great-grandfather.

"I wouldn't marry that red-faced, puffy-eyed,
blubbery creature!" bawled the young man.

"I certainly wouldn't marry that muddy, clumsy oaf!"
sobbed Valentine.

Great-grandfather called a special meeting.
"They seem a perfect pair," he said,
"but they'll not have each other.
What can we do?"

"He's not going anywhere for a while
with that broken toe," said Valentine's mothers.

"Let's just wait and see what happens," said her fathers.

"The way to a man's heart is through his stomach,"
said her grandmothers.

"Feed him," said her grandfathers.
"We will," said her brothers and sisters.
So they did.

Fortunately, they could.
Valentine's crying had caused the gardens
to grow as gigantic as her tears.

The young man was kept comfortable
and well fed by the villagers,
but he was bored with just sitting and
waiting for his toe to heal.
He began talking to Valentine.
He told her of his travels
and his loneliness.

Valentine was so bored that she listened.
As she listened she began to smile.
Perhaps he wasn't such a clumsy oaf after all.
When Valentine smiled, the young man realized
how beautiful she really was.

By the time his toe healed
the young man and Valentine had become
absolutely silly about each other.

"Marry me, Valentine. I love you, dearly,"
said the young man.

"I love you too, but I can't marry you!"
said Valentine. And she started to sob and bawl
like the baby she had been.

Great-grandfather called a special meeting.

"Why won't she marry him?" he wanted to know.

"We'll ask her," said her mothers.

"Ask her quick before we all drown!" said her fathers.

"I can't marry him because I haven't a thing to wear!"
wailed Valentine. And it was true.
They hadn't been able to manage anything large enough
for her to wear for years.

"I see the problem," said Great-grandfather.

"A girl can't get married in her birthday suit!"

"She certainly can't," said Valentine's fathers.

"It wouldn't be proper," said her grandmothers.

"It would be chilly," said her grandfathers.

"We'll just have to make her a wedding dress!"
said her brothers and sisters.
So they did.

Valentine and her sweetheart were married on February 14.

It was a very large, beautiful wedding.

Great-grandfather performed the ceremony.

Valentine's fathers gave the bride away.

Her mothers cried.

Valentine's grandmothers baked the cake.

Her grandfathers made the music.

Her brothers and sisters danced and sang,

and everyone was merry.

After the wedding
Great-grandfather called a special meeting.
"I have decided that we will celebrate Valentine's Day
every February 14 from now on," he declared.

"Of course!" agreed Valentine's family.

So they did.